metamorphosis:

purple butterflies dance to jazz

Jacqueline T. Hill

DEDICATION

This book is dedicated to my parents, sister, two favorite nieces, great-nephew, Mamie Carr, Teresa Sepaugh, Clarice Bledsoe, and the late Toni Morrison.

CONTENTS

Hugo Dos Santos' Note

A few years back, a great reader and better friend cautioned me about the danger of feeling like I should (could?) only write about the Newark neighborhood where I grew up. It was wise advice that came from someone who had read a lot of my work. I didn't act on that suggestion, but it marked me.

In the years between then and now I've thought about that conversation at least once a week. And there have been weeks and weeks where I've thought about it daily. It probably goes without saying that I think about it more often when I am in the process of writing.

If you're at all familiar with my work, you know that I have written about Newark quite a bit. The act of writing is a private enterprise and in the privacy of my thoughts I am always revisiting my old neighborhood, re-walking those streets. I've written about other people and places, too, for sure. But if I were to take an inventory of every word I've written creatively the final tally would show that I have written overwhelmingly about the same place and the same people. I didn't plan for this, nor have I tried to avoid it. I have simply allowed my writing to follow the vein of my interests.

I include this personal anecdote here because while I believe that good writers can force their hands to write about topics that are removed from their interests, I also believe that doing so does not usually yield the best writing. The best writing, writing that reveals and affects, is most commonly, and in my experience, the result of good writers pursuing their interests.

Some interests are obvious. Others are hidden from us. Sometimes we find them but mostly they find us.

Jacqueline's work actively investigates the faraway corners of her interests. Even interests she might have once kept at a distance. And along that journey she has changed. She hasn't become different — she has become more. She has found a way to own that which once confined her. She has evolved.

Her book is a testament to that evolution, an evolution that came after plenty of reflection and personal struggle, and I am so proud of her for pursuing her passion. I am proud to call her a friend. May we all be brave enough to pursue that which we perceive to be bigger than us.

Hugo dos Santos
Flemington (not Newark), August 2019

Introduction

I love writing. I'm the writer who pours her heart into words to tell stories readers will relate to and connect with while reading them. These poems and short stories came to life during my undergrad years between 2002 and 2005. They were tucked away deep within the shallow depths of my soul and "chrysalis." I did not know these words existed in my mind until my college professors challenged me. Hence, their push-backs began my metamorphosis.

At first glance, my experience strictly aligns with the meaning of metamorphosis. I underwent a (mental) process by which my thinking and writing developed through a new "birth" or "hatching," involving a "conspicuous and relatively abrupt change in its structure through growth and differentiation."

While trapped in the chrysalis, "the old body parts of a caterpillar transforming," I could feel convictions for writing from an authentic place in my heart. Interestingly, I didn't have these convictions in my parent's home. My parents invested and enrolled me in the proper schools to nurture my creative gifts.

They noticed my gifts to sing, play instruments, dance, and write poems. Moreover, these jewel's put me in front of reputable teachers and mentors to grow and cultivate my abilities. However, as I grew older and learned things from the traditional church, specific convictions constrained me to change my lifestyle. I feared not living a "godly" life. Therefore, I hid all of my gifts.

While attending mandatory, creative writing classes in college, confusion about what to write and how to write it became my worst enemy. My writings were the only ones in class to talk about God, reference the bible and church. My classmates would write alluring poems and short stories from authentic connections to their experiences. They weren't afraid to write about sex, alcohol, parties, and mere life enjoyments.

I remember barely scratching the surface of the blank canvas. Feeling limited and restricted due to religious practices and training from the church. Sex-talk, questioning, living, and writing "secularly" was a no-no. It's taboo and hushed with a holy seal. Convictions gripped my heart, fears flooded my soul, and inner-being because of too many constraints.

Something had to give. So, I decided to take the leap and shift my thinking with the help of my college professors and other notable writers. I put my trust in their guidance, lectures, and teachings.

My writing comes from the chrysalis to the page due to a liberating experience in my Intermediate Creative Writing and Advanced poetry classes while in undergrad. Both Paul Genega and Patrick Rosal played intricate roles in my freedom.

Sometimes the right people enter your life to challenge you and your writings enough to pull out the best in you. These perfect teachers prepared me for the world of writing. Thus, they instilled the best motivation for daily writing. Both classes were eclectic with challenges and dared potential writers to take many risks to be transparent. It taught me how to write prose and verse freely.

Writing from the heart requires freedom. Being liberated to write from the heart is righteous. The prolific writer, Alice Walker, once said,

The most healthy thing is to be true to your own self, quoting—who was it, Hamlet?—but also, that you have a right to express what you see and what you feel and what you think. To be bold. To be as bold with your vision as you can possibly be.

She's right. I have every right to say and include in my writings anything I want. Writing from a real place in the heart allows people to connect with you better. People can feel authenticity and realness, just like you and me. And, when you're walking and writing from a place of freedom, nothing means more than this.

Allow me to explain what this means for my heart and life. I feel freedom. I'm free from fears and the constraints of religious chains and dogmas that tell you not to think like the "world." Guess this means they have the power to take my "salvation" according to their definition, standards, and terms of the agreement.

I now have new sanity and salvation on the sexiest blank canvases every morning. We have a continuous intimacy of love creating–creations of real tongue-talking climaxes. I love every drip and drop of being fluid-like silky velvet. So, I've destroyed what some believe would cause me to go astray. Writing from the heart didn't prevent me from becoming an incredible writer of nonfiction and fiction.

Here's the beauty of it all. Writing, coupled with its genres are alluring. I now understand how many writers use their gifts. And only feel gripped with anxieties and lack of motivation when they can't write or express themselves however they choose.

When I finally let go of the boundaries, as I released the brakes of religion, I began to read, critique, and model the works of Toni Morrison, bell hooks, Zora Neale Hurston, Langston Hughes, Patrick Rosal, Amy Tan, Maya Angelou,

Nikki Giovanni, plus many more. I began to write on an elevated level, which involves applying many crafting techniques.

After looking at other works of fiction from such incredible writers, I learned how to apply similar styles to my craft. My eyes are keen and able to recognize literary techniques. The mechanics of fiction has enabled me to efficiently develop characters, foreshadowing, point of view, theme, tone, atmosphere, etc.

Verse, on the other hand, taught how to use metaphors, similes, rhyme, enjambment, wordplay, alliteration, stanza breaks, rhythm, and more. These techniques continue to perfect my writing. I feel secure. I have a beautifully adorned blanket over my heart-writings for safety. I am ready for the world of writers, as I have developed my style and feel confident.

Preface

The assembled works in this book consists of two short stories: The Dark Promise and The Grudge, and 13 poems: *Lost & Found, I Ponder This, Gospel According to Jazz, I Hate Going, Jill Wishes, Still Working, Directions, The Sanctioned Dream, If I Were At West Kinney Street, Dancing with Fred, Metamorphosis, Reflections*, plus more.

One poem focuses on writing from the omniscience perspective. This style shows a story with two or more characters revealing the mind of all. The same technique can also be of use in limited omniscience, which only tells the mind of one character, usually the protagonist. In my story, "Christina's Benefits," I applied limited omniscience. I also employed an atmosphere centered around the antagonist to help unfold both inner and outer conflicts.

This setup increased the tone of deception throughout the story. I intentionally set anticipation so the reader would eventually believe that the antagonist was involved in another relationship with a physical person. The protagonist has a loud voice because the story tells from her point of view. The use of character development was employed to learn the personality of each character. The reader would be able to clearly depict both characters persona.

In "The Grudge," my primary focus was punctuation, atmosphere and tone. The atmosphere begins calm and then provoked to aggravation. The tone begins with laugher, giddiness, fun and settlement. Due to the large amount of dialogue, the use of correct punctuation was necessary.

Verse, or poetry is where I began to employ many literary techniques because of my security in writing it. The ten poems in this portfolio include use of metaphors, similes, rhyme, enjambment, punctuation, figurative language, word play, alliteration, repetition, stanza breaks, rhythm, and long/short line usage.

The Gospel According to Jazz, (A tribute to the late artist Jackson Pollock's piece Autumn Rhythm), was my favorite piece, as I feel this has unleashed my gift of writing from fears. This type of free-verse doesn't limit the writer, and its form can be written in any style. The crafting of *The Gospel According to Jazz,* and the free flow of the poem is what allows interpretation to the actual piece of artwork. This expresses a free-spirit of contour lines always intersecting and never stopping, as with free-verse writing, which includes the usage of enjambment- lines running over. It enhances the flow and rhythm of the poem. As the painting is constantly moving, the poem keeps up with its speed.

"Jill Wishes" is a poem where I employed word play and rhyme. I took an end-rhyme, internal rhyme approach and used shorter lines for the rhythm of the poem. –Trying to keep the same nursery rhyme feel *of Jack and Jill went up the hill…* Through this, I have learned that shorter lines will move the flow and reading of the poem faster, and longer lines will slow it down. This same technique was applied to "Still Working." The difference in this poem is there is no rhyme. The lines are still short, as it provokes the feel of a hectic workday. Here, I employed repetition with words. The other poems in this portfolio reflect the usage of metaphors, figurative language, etc. I enjoyed writing with those techniques. However, I believe that my poetic strengths are in short lines, repetition, word play, enjambment, etc.

You are about to journey through an array of other poems. Some of the enclosed writings will require you to walk slowly, while with others you must walk quickly. Thus, as you walk, listen to its rhythms, -its music, and -how every line is related to the meaning Metamorphosis. The boundary of every line releases energy of love, hurt, and venom. These qualities were like vitamins. They entered into my blood stream. So rather than give in, they gave me the speed and endurance to pursue my destiny for writing, and I became stronger to carry my destiny. As stated above, I developed tenacity for an unthinkable goal. As the above energies traveled swiftly through me, they became a strong hold, too.

I had come to the realization that this was winning half the battle.

The poems in this book demonstrate weaknesses that have been shifted into strengths. They show the ability to write outside of the box. As well as, how to develop a technical pattern. At first, writing poems was not clear to me. I did not fully understand all of the technicalities. I was not sure where to add end-stops, line-breaks, syntax, etc. For a minute, I felt so lost, but writing daily; and taking classes with Pat and Paul helped me tremendously. Now, I am more secure in writing. I feel more comfortable with writing. As aforementioned, I was provoked to write. I was pushed - forced -and had no choice. I do not mind sharing what little I have written. I hope you enjoy my blend of experiences that are now transferred from my memory, to the hand, through the pen, and now for the public eye to read.

Overall, I enjoyed writing these poems and forming a book for them. Now, I find myself reading other materials and applying new crafting techniques. I feel very confident and at ease with writing. It is a technique that I really enjoy. Today, I'm a purple butterfly dancing to riffs and runs from jazzy sounds and scatting penned to the page. Dance with me. I want you to take pleasure in this new dance.

Metamorphosis

Time rewinds forward

Think backwards to

Our love falling in

One heart open

The other shut

Down for non-repair

Spirals down to one

Chance only to

Marry and carry

Love alone through

One chrysalis at a

Time rewinds up

Towards nothing

Leaves for something

More Beautiful.

Lost & Found (Re-Thinking Hugo Dos Santos)

Ten years ago we

conversed everyday

Three months ago

I was reunited with

thoughts about him

And only one hour ago

I realized this empty-perplexed

moment raped my hunger and

thirst for his under

standing and now I'm

imagining him

there, naked, vital

to time and space--

things I hallucinate about

Now I think

of his crisp smoothness

and all that he

allows me to say through silence

Only scratching can be

heard as I tattoo his

smooth skin, his unbending

and unyielding urge to

give in under my command

He is where I find my sanity and salvation; the page

The Dark Promise

The choir members marched down the aisle in royal purple and white with puffy sleeves and long flowing heavenly robes. Sister Flowers swayed offbeat, just like every Sunday. I conducted a song that particular Sunday. And I noticed how Xavier sat in the pulpit's wine-colored, cherry wood chair. He kept eyeing me up and down. Each time, I saw him staring at my toes. I wore these Cinderella glass-looking heels with open toes. A French manicure alluringly dressed my toes. I blushed, and my heart started beating fast. I already knew he was interested. I could feel it. He could feel it.

Xavier pushed through the crowd to greet me after service. I continued speaking with Sister Marilyn about her solo. She always had trouble remembering the words to her songs. Everyone else around me rushed to greet Reverend Jones. I. Saw. Xavier. Our eyes locked. He made his way closer to me. Damn! Why did his cologne lull me into a trance? Does he know women fall for Dolce & Gabanna?

"Well, hello there," Xavier remarked in this silky, Barry White voice.

"Hello," I responded looking at my toes and twiddling my fingers.

"Great service, right?"

"Yes! It really was awesome! Rev. surely preached an on-time word!"

"Well... looks like God sent me on time for your number."

"I'd love to call you sometime."

He reached for his pen inside his suit jacket. I looked around to see if anyone noticed our interaction. Especially, Sis Flowers who knew everybody's business and told everybody's business.

"Duh?! Why am I reaching for my pen when we have phones for this?" he said.

"Ummmm, I wondered the same."

We laughed. In this very moment, we knew there was a deep connection beyond our control. Could it be God? I mean, our flirting took place in the pulpit. You know, God's "holy place." We exchanged numbers and quickly tucked away our phones like professionals.

"Thank you, Sister Williams. You'll hear from me this week," he said.

Take a deep breath girl. You heard him correctly. Don't call him first though. Let him call you.

The next day at work, I arrive from lunch at my desk. Before I sat down, the front area reception called. "Ms. Williams, there's a delivery for you. Are you coming to pick it up, or should I send it to you?"

"I'll come down," I said. As I approached the front desk, I saw a stunning, pink rose arrangement.

"These are for you!" the receptionist said.

"Why, thank you," I replied.

My coworkers stared at the floral arrangement. I could hear their whispering. And, of course, everyone wants to know who sent them. I'm not dating anyone. I sat at my desk and opened the card attached to the flowers.

You are so beautiful to me.

Who sent me these roses? No one signed the card. I looked to see who owned the floral shop to get a number to call. An instant Google search with "The Perfect Day Floral" got the phone number in two seconds. I called.

"This is Perfect Day Floral. How may I help you?"

"Yes, I'm Christine! I received a floral arrangement at The Stargazell Newspaper at 12:30 PM. Can you please tell me the name of the sender?"

"Sure, Ms. Chrissss... Christine Williams?"

"Yes."

"I'm sorry, dear! I've been asked to not give this information."

"Wow! Okay, thank you!"

"Well, ain't this 'bout a son of a bih. I hope these aren't from Jayden. This cat always pops up at the oddest seasons," I say shaking my head.

The workday comes to an end. I'm tired. Exhausted. I hope no one calls me to hang out after work. My girlfriends love hanging out even when it's not happy hour.

RING! RING! Who's calling me now? Unknown number??? I'm looking at my phone wondering if I should answer or not.

"Hello?"

"Hey, gorgeous!"

"Oh, hey."

"You know who this is?"

"Ummm, are we really playing the guessing game?"

"My bad, hon! It's Jayden."

I hang up without a care in the world. This cat is bad news, and I'm not for his drama or BS today. Another call beeps in from another unknown number.

This just can't be happening right.

"Hello?! Who is this?"

"Oh. Did I catch you at a bad time?"

"What's with people playing detective these..."

"Hold on, dear. It's me, Xavier. Are you having a good day?"

I look at my phone in awe. My heart starts beating fast like a woman making love to her man. I begin to daydream about him. About us.

"Ahem. Hello, are you there?"

Swallowing my heart back down my throat, I respond, "Yes."

We have an amazing conversation during my drive home. I park my car, gather my things and get out; we're still talking.

"Xavier, can I call you back after I get settled here?" He responds, "Sure! I'll be waiting by the phone."

I call back two hours later. His mom answers the phone. Our start doesn't go too well. She replies with this rigidly cold voice and asks who's calling. I tell her who I am. "Xavier, some white girl is on the phone for you," she yells. White girl? Did she just call me the W word? This is gonna be an interesting ride.

Our conversation goes pretty smoothly. There's an alluring exchange. You can tell we're feeling each other. The night grows late. We talk about our food likes and dislikes, types of restaurants albeit independent or chain, favorite colors, and then.

"So, how do you like your flowers," he asked.

"Wait. You sent me these roses?, I inquired.

"Yes. Did you notice there are twenty-three pinks and one white,"

"Honestly, I didn't count them. I was too amazed and awestruck by them. What made you send them?"

"Your beauty says it all, and you're so pure--kinda innocent."

"Kinda..."

"Yes. You've lived a little, right?" He chuckled.

"I guess you're right."

Yawning. I look at the clock as it turns to 11:59 p.m. I still haven't prepared myself for work. I've completed nothing this evening. No lunch. No clothes ironed. Haven't removed my make-up all day. Boy, this will cause the making of a few pimples. Oily-skin doesn't help any when mixed with wearing foundation, blush, concealer, etc. up till almost midnight.

"Well, I should probably go now. I need to get ready for work tomorrow."

"Yeah. I don't want you to go. But, I understand. How about we talk more tomorrow? It just so happens to be Friday."

"Sure."

"I'll call you tomorrow evening. I promise."

"I look forward to it, sweetie!"

We hang up the phone. I turn on the radio and rush to get myself together for work. At this rate, I'm only going to get six hours of sleep. One of my favorite songs comes on, "Butta Love" by the group Next. I'm already emotional. Attached. It didn't take long. Butterflies in my belly. I can't stop thinking of him.

I think of his height--that 5'11" frame. His physique is absolutely everything. He has well-toned muscles. They show through his suits. He has caramel, evenly toned skin. No blemishes. Smooth and sexy chestnut eyes. This cat even has a sexy butt. I mean... Oh, Lord, please be a fence around my thoughts. I can't stop thinking of him.

Over the course of the next three months, Xavier became acquainted with my mother and family. He purposely moved slowly, like he was hiding something from me. Eventually he asked if I was ready to be exclusive.

We would spend evenings in New York under the electrifying lights of Time Square. Every Thursday we had date nights that seemed to last forever. We talked on the phone nonstop, night and day. Jayden and I finally became exclusive and it felt too good to be true. One evening I called him as usual so we could decide on a time to meet, but the call went to voicemail. It's our sixth month anniversary. He called back after getting off from work. "I'm coming to the house," he said. It's his usual routine. But, 6 PM, no Xavier. 7 PM, where is he? 8:30 PM, still no Xavier. I started to worry, so I called his mother.

"Hi, Mrs. Howell! It's Christine."

"Hey, dear, how are you?"

"Oh, I'm hanging in there. Is Xavier there?"

"No dear. I thought he was with you. Did you try his cell?"

"Yes, I did. No response though."

"Call me back sweetheart in a few hours if you still don't hear from him."

"Ok, will do!"

11:30 PM, no Xavier. I call his mom back and hear this strict motherly tone say, "CHRISTINE, LEAVE MY SON ALONE. HE IS NO GOOD!" Listening to this was not easy for me to accept. Xavier was gone for three days. He did not report to work, nor did he call me. Our Thursday night was ruined for the first time. Xavier gets paid every Thursday night. I remember clearly because that's how we were able to do many things for date nights. By now, he has me wrapped around his finger and knew it. I believed he loved me as much as I loved him. But something didn't feel right. My stomach started to feel knots form in it.

I called his mom again and she gave me the address to go to Xavier. I arrived on Christopher Street and I parked my car in front of a white and black house. I knocked on the door and it opened enough to get me inside. I went downstairs and found Xavier using broken straws to feel the high from pharmaceuticals through white powders. Come to find out he's been addicted to powders for years. He had this recreational adrenaline the whole time. I found the nose of Xavier embedded in the reflection of a silver mirror. Xavier looked up at me vaguely, as though unsure of who I was. He only had eyes for the supernatural. Sweat ran profusely down his face. Blinking, he realized who I was.

I endured the trauma of knowing about his habit for a year, - tried to help him and be there. Constantly picking him up after every disappearance-sometimes even beat to death. He never laid a finger on me, but the emotional abuse was just as bad. Valentine's Day, I ended our relationship.

I Ponder This

Recognition that erases virtue

from the mind of these words

spoken to mouths to see what I say

lost in layers of white space.

Silence absorbed loudly in your eyes

purged with hyssop before released to soar

and cry sad-happy smiles

from the wisdom of Solomon

which exceeds folly, as light excels darkness.

Being like a tree planted by rivers of waters

bringing forth abundant fruit in due season.

The Gospel According To Jazz: Tribute to Jackson Pollock's Autumn Rhythm

Pulls blues out the right hip

funk from the left thigh

-makes ya move to the

rhythm of the beat

from the horse's feet

snap your fingers to the

groove of

     smooth

         moved

              soothed riffs

from ebony runs and ivory's swift

quick tickle of pricked keys

A flat G sharp trends

illuminating artists

inspiring paint to

run to and fro

mirroring black and white

with a splash of blue notes

aimed to reveal

the concealed mind of one

spiritual

     literal

          mystical

               musical

mental thinking hand.

that recorded nature in Autumn Rhythm

I Hate Going...

Here I am again
in literature class sitting
looking, waiting to hear
of another screw up from management
possible mess up on schedules that
mirror true disorganization from
dysfunctional minds who teach
us teachers to complain and explain
explain and complain about the
same bullshit which occurs every year,
semester, mid-term and final
indirectly pouring meetings before
dawn and at sun set I'm
ready to pack-up and go
go home and come back

again to meet at 8:30 a.m.

in rooms full of priests-professors

lecturing the class on mentalities

they should have

in an institution full of 4.0's

but are brainless to common knowledge.

.

Jill Wishes

He loved her like

butter pecan ice cream

chocolate deluxe

melting

in rays sun beams

screams pleasured

pains subsiding

tumbling between

grass and leaves

yellows and greens

caress this goddess

being like

licking vanilla beans

before dropping

then rising to

climaxed realms

calling deep to

depths of a sea

saw motioning

before releasing

waters

waters connecting

seas to shiny seas

to conceive babies

linking him back to

her dreams

ish realities of

sexing Jill on a hill

Jane spills thrills

hooking him to

her for eternity..

If I were at West Kinney Street Projects,

I'd sing about the mini broken -powdered glass tubes,
shattered windows
crushed dreams
brick city tattooed all over with graffiti
defeated -high class weed smoking cocaine graduates
addicts of a slow dance to the ground from the sound of
music so loud
hip hop you don't stop with *Bonita Applebaum*,
Sex You Up, Check the Rhyme, -Groove Me
listen to smoke from rocks
watch children play when they're really asleep
in empty rooms where we whispered with boys
-introduced to the ghetto by Shamika
the secret I forgot....

Dancing

Let's count--
One. Two. One-Two-Three.
One-Two-Three.

Baby, your so smooth
I love to see you groove
Swinging out, dancing 'bout
You've got that snap, dab
Bounce, swinging side-to-side
You glide
Lookin sexy wanna ride
Your lap this time-- I Like

I like the way you
Groove it and move it

Doin 'your thing

Doin 'your swing

Lookin 'classy

Lookin 'sexy

I like the way you

Move it and groove it

Let's count--

One. Two. One-Two-Three.

One-Two-Three.

First Awakening

The journey seemed long

traveled from ocean to land

and found myself wrapped in layers of

cotton first from blankets then to

arms that passed me from her to

him who delivered me out of the

basket which flowed down a river

that passed through a tight

valley and eventually parted like the red

sea from the command of the rod

in his hand and instruction of wisdom

in his mouth this coached her into

my safe arrival then kissed by

a smack to my behind that

opened my eyes which reverted

me back to the river

-this time it flowed from my eyes

and they fell into the cup

of her lips and cheeks

I hushed with my eyes wide shut

and laid there awake--finally.

Directions

Drive eyes south

Pass over the hill of the nose

Merge into the curves of his mouth

U-Turns tongues with prose

Make slight right

Yield to his lead

Proceed at red light

Stay in the middle lane, he'll plead

I am between

the depths of exchange, destination of new

the shallowness of things

this kiss in a box for you.

Reflections

Mother like mirrors

comes round to tell me truth

Listen, she said

    (I keep my eye focused on the poor old man

    who comes every Sunday for a taste of happiness)

Continue to be a leader not a follower. You'll escaped the patterned curse - same

bloodline in your father. You're my likeness and image of survival

    (It's Sunday again and he sneaks out before I see him.

    I perform my routines, look my self in the mirror…)

    Watch for them that creep in houses. May lead you astray. Some way seem

right, but

It will lead to death. That enemy comes to kill, steal and destroy.

(... which is my shade to block reality. There is only he and me.

but now, just me)

Stand. Endure hardness. Light affliction is good. It's here but for a moment.

(Veins like broken mirrors seem even brighter under

the early morning light, says the old man).

Look not to what is seen, it's temporary. What is not seen is forever. This will

exceed a far more weight of honor, which will reflect in your works

(Come back with more, the old man said, But my sympathy is my goal with this $20.

I have my temporary rush of happiness now, he uttered).

Eye sees the I in him.

Reflects the him in Eye.

Still Working

Sun rises light and sweet

morning is here

there

near

far

everywhere

all around

men begin to labor there

here for hours

far from home

near to inmates

who contemplate

conjure

manipulate

scheme to

build up sweat from

brows in forms of

blood from machines

here

there

near

everywhere in corporations

businesses small

there worked over

paid under

here

beats tock-tick

pressured damnation

plastic consequences

for work unfinished

displayed

there

by morning headlines

everywhere reports elsewhere

here reports nowhere

threats and threats from

mere man

controlled by the boss

from the boss's boss

here

where

clocks keep and tell time

 everywhere

but keeps still truths

never revealed

so shrug off the future

and leave it in the past

'cause the present is all new

here

there

near

everywhere

the sun will never set.

The Sanctioned Dream (Rethinking A Song from *The Canterville Ghost* Stage Play)

Am I living a dream?

Are my eyes closed to reality?

Are your soft spoken words

mistakenly heard, smiles meant for me?

Am I living a dream? Should my eyes be opened wide?

Will you just fade away,

or even stay for me?

A new and everlasting love could grow.

Showered blessings will always flow

like a gentle stream without any theme.

Am I living a dream?

Should my eyes be opened wide

in this dream sanctioned for love?

Is it a haven for trust?

In sleep we meet, see I to I

mirroring our inner-conflicts

of virtue and adoration

mesmerized through our eyes

It's where this metamorphosis manifests

from inward to outward revealing

the super in natural, each drip in the drops

of our soul becoming whole and bold bursting from illusions

This can't be a dream.

It seems too dim,

too dark for light, yet

too heavenly for hell

Let's sleep again

Wake to this dream

Let's meet again

To be caught up in our rapture

-the reality, the sanctuary, not nightmares.

The Grudge

Choir rehearsal was longer than usual. The RPM choir practiced two hours every Thursday, but for some reason Brother Ralph Pollock just couldn't catch the intro of the song. He would begin singing prior to the timing of his cue, which threw the entire choir off, including the director. Everyone left the choir stand in frustration. Some mumbled. Others complained. Then there was Sister Aretha Williams, who walked down the choir stairs, laughing and singing from today's song, "I'm going home to drink some water from the fountain."

"Well, I'm going to rest from my labor," Sister Ann Watts proclaimed to Sister Williams, following behind her. The other choir members laughed so hard they had stomach pains. Meanwhile, Brother Pollock was highly offended and stormed to his car.

My mother and I were driving home still reminiscing about rehearsal and Brother Pollock. Rolling down the window, 72 degrees of air smacked me in the face. Approaching a light, a jet-black Mercedes was blasting "Sex You Up." The guys and girls hanging out on the corner were dancing with 40s, swinging from side to side in rhythm to the music. Driving along Lyons Avenue is truly a treat in itself.

"Ma, look! There's Aunty Marilyn in front of us," I said, popping up in my seat.

"It sure is," she responded.

"Let's play a trick on her," I said. During this time, we stopped at the red light between Lyons Avenue and Union Avenue. Looking through the windshield, I could see my aunt snapping her fingers in the air, bobbing and dancing to the same song. So my mother eased up and bumped her car. My aunt began screaming and hollering and made an illegal left turn to get to the Parkway.

Of course, my mom and I were laughing hysterically all the way home. We began talking about how Aunt Marilyn and our family played jokes with each other from time to time. When we walked through the door, the phone rang. It was Aunt Marilyn.

"Hello."

"Oh my, Lord!!! This is Aunty Marilyn. Is your mother or father home?" she asked nervously with panic in her voice.

"Hold on. Ma, telephone! It's Aunt Marilyn," I said, snickering.

"Hey, Marilyn."

"Jackie! Where's Nate? I was at the light on the corner of Lyons and Union Avenue and a car rear-ended me."

She asked for my father because, at the time, he was a Narcotics Detective for Newark.

"Marilyn, Nate's at work. Besides that was Tee and I who bumped your car while you were dancing and all," my Mother uttered. Before we knew it, Aunty Marilyn hung up the phone. She didn't speak to the family for 2 months.

New-A-Mentry

4" grade ends

Promoted to 5'''

familiar faces

familiar friends

down with the trends

now must go

pushed to a new institute

 grades talked

music talent exposed—my gifts

which walked me

to the place that

expresses, -possesses, -stresses

 the importance of art

the hidden jewel of

my renaissance endowed

in this era.

Round 1

2:58 p.m. tick tock

time runs forward

sweat drops like

blood from my

forehead, hands tremble

drop to my

thighs and shake—

legs race up

and down stirs

up a rhythm

as a drum

roll this girl

big as Wonder

Woman me, frail

as olive oil

the bell rings

student scatter like

roaches from their

seats to the

big concrete arena

rather than double-dutch

the fight begins

of course I

won, but the

games had just begun.

Communication

Lips struggle
Tongue explores the mouth
Cries choke back strange syllables
I'd rather write it down.

Words unreleased,
fear of laughter, -this new language
fear of words —intimidated by verbs-
I'd rather be silent.

My native is **English**
My tongue **afiada**, the construct of my being
My language is not common to you
I'd rather be home.

Little One

She is so delicate

Inside is where she hides,

this is her haven, safety —protection.

Not high maintenance —

for a moment she is happy, but then

reverts back to the secret place.

Giving unto others, she neglects

the honey she craves

barren, yet does not abandon the milk

she needs for nourishment.

As Judas betrayed Jesus with a kiss,

she can relate

will she befriend again?

Timid — wolves in sheep clothing raped her innocence.

She deserted the arc of safety, but for a season —

She found the whole of love,

the acquaintance was manipulation —

the lover was deceit.

Raised in depths of morals, heights of values-

Strayed, now has detoured to the inner being.

Inside is where she hides

this is her haven, safety —protection.

A developed woman just in time

know how to reach her now.

know where to find her now.

I Remember the Room

where giggles and friendship hugged the

atmosphere and unfolded from the

abundance of our hearts to seal the

covenant of a bond released through comfort

in trust of each other. I, closer to you than

a brother loved at all times in action and

deed through uncle sam's green

blessed you with milk and honey. Until

one day, my right hand discerned you were

the enemy who whispered secrets I innocently

locked in your loins 'cause jealousy and envy

became god's of your heart. Now the room once

alive is dead from the bitter commune with the

green eye companion I was traded for.

No Excuse

Warfare has trespassed

determined to win this war

between my enemy called "flesh" and

my friend called "righteousness" thus rudimentary

skills still spill from clay lips of mom,

how her voice echoes in the corner of mind.

Though I hear words in secret places of thunder

 this thorn in my flesh still lingers.

When alone it hides behind the members of my body.

But, then once he came the covers were pulled.

A picture taken, -instantly

immobile. Tried to wait.

Wanted to become Mrs., first.

Betwixt and caught

in the core of his game.

Her voice still rings in my inner

ears. This thrill is nourishment,

which I can't neglect.

It was my first taste of strawberries and chocolate with sex.

Eden

I noticed you before you noticed me-

-your skin as pure- as clear water-

-your smile, -it was brighter than white-

-your voice —anointed like a burning bush

And your form, made in the image and likeness-

of a God I have never seen-

have yet to see, -under the layers of your clothes what-

His invisible hands have created. —But t can imagine — barely.-

I ponder your hands so strong yet so soft, -how they welcomed me

into your embrace. —The sensitive power of your arms - released me to

a place of safety -home —belonging —love-

A place marked by so many levels of passion, -waters I could drown in –

dying of love.- Or live, baptized anew.

By the way, -may I kiss you again

embrace the manhood of your lips,

feel the power of life through you

until I become breathless —powerless —from

 your masculinity

We are approaching pure unity

 -the rhythm of two hearts beating as one

As Adam was asleep with one rib removed —the other placed

in Eve, I am your other rib —the one who has awakened you.

When I haven't been kissed in a long time

I hear music up above my head
 so loud I still hear your lips sing for mine.

Listen to black keys pecked
Your tongue riffs like white keys on my neck
your lips melody and rhyme
in the G clef of my mouth--
-modulate-
from d flat to c sharp baby, there is no
 -difference the key remains the same
as your kiss, -an octave from my name.

No Rest

Darkness was brighter than light
my eyes adjusted to the rays of night
only to see an image, - a person, -the soul,
 -a spirit of peaceful caution.

As she treads, night lingers in every
step of the day. The sun dies when she is
present. Her shadow absorbs the
 bright of the moon.

She tramps softly to my bedside,
to discover my rest. Anger journeys
to the seat of her breast. Whispers
for help, she beckons them by name

one by one, they surround me

fear, torment and perfect hate.

I call the word, he does not hear me

I call for truth, he does not sustain me

Now I awake with sweet pain

Mom nor Dad hears me call their name

The spirit -is now my strong hold

No rest for her, -silent torment for my soul.

Swift & Strong

Strong…

    Fear & wonderfully

made strategically joint 2-gether

mixed in a swirl of black & white

with a pinch of Indian tribe added

to enhance the perfection of my

cheeks both on face and the other place.

Dainty in size

exquisite in conduct. A lady

with class, elegance

excellence, confidence, importance.

Perpetual growth, augmented maturation

stole the man right before your eyes

he took your precious, I still have mine

my head is lifted up, yours is down

provoked —invoked —stroked nothing sways me

I'm a leader, not a follower into destiny

Identified as

Swift...

in this race, as I can endure

all hardships —moving at a fast pace

lock into position as an eagle for take off

and quickly soar through the storms ahead

shred down the tares _the blades of barren

fields. I'll run slow- walk into leaps —and

skip into tomorrow-listen quickly and —

speak slowly. Thus the sun and moon

will stand still as I win this battle.

The Moment

Beyond ready

forced to Shift into

external life

a world unknown, -unfamiliar.

Born in sin —Shaped in iniquity

from a womb which travailed tears

of pain —discomfort.

Kidnapped from safety

Seize the moment

Introduced to arrows by night and day

of those who are foes —betrayers —deceivers.

I have cried. Life has ended.

-And I am buried into

newness -utopia —eternal life,

The foes, betrayers, and deceivers will lead to

the hidden treasures found in the darkness of this world.

Through them I learned how to be a friend

-how to trust, -how to kiss, -how to love, -how to obtain joy.

Life begins.

ABOUT THE AUTHOR

Jacqueline T. Hill is the author of nine books, a ghostwriter and content writer. She blogs weekly on short stories, poems, self-improvement, writing tips, and education. Her writings have been featured in Bloomfield Blink Literary Ink, the Top 25 Social Media Marketing, and other publications. Jacqueline has an M.Div from Drew University and M.Ed in Educational Leadership & Administration from Northcentral University. She works in administration for public schools at the secondary level.

Visit her website at ***www. thelivingacts.com***

www.ingramcontent.com/pod-product-compliance
Lightning Source LLC
Chambersburg PA
CBHW071203130626
46555CB00004B/1560